Thomas K. Serrano

Saved from the Wreck

A Drama in Three Acts

Thomas K. Serrano

Saved from the Wreck
A Drama in Three Acts

ISBN/EAN: 9783337343149

Printed in Europe, USA, Canada, Australia, Japan

Cover: Foto ©Andreas Hilbeck / pixelio.de

More available books at **www.hansebooks.com**

SAVED FROM THE WRECK

A DRAMA

IN THREE ACTS

BY

THOMAS K SERRANO

———

PRINTED FROM THE AUTHOR'S MANUSCRIPT WITH THE CAST OF THE CHAR-
ACTERS SYNOPSIS OF INCIDENTS TIME OF REPRESENTATION COSTUMES
SCENE AND PROPERTY PLOTS DIAGRAMS OF THE STAGE SET-
TINGS SIDES OF ENTRANCE AND EXIT RELATIVE POSI-
TIONS OF THE PERFORMERS EXPLANATION OF
THE STAGE DIRECTIONS TABLEAUX ETC
AND ALL OF THE STAGE BUSINESS

———

———

NEW YORK
HAROLD ROORBACH, PUBLISHER
9 MURRAY STREET

SAVED FROM THE WRECK.

CAST OF CHARACTERS.

FAYETTE ATWOOD, - - - A country squire.
JOSEPH LATOUR, A gentleman of means, "Saved from the Wreck."
AUGUSTUS GIGGLE, - - Whose nature resembles his name.
CLINCHER KATCRAFT, - Keeper of the light-house at Barnegat.
HARLEY, - - - - - Assistant at the light-house.
MICHAEL MULLIN, { An individual whose hands have a preposses-
sion for other people's pockets.
SAMMY, - - - - - - A light-house assistant.
TEDDY FIZZLES, { A detective who does not always act on the
information he receives.
MADELINE, - " - - - - Squire Atwood's wife.
NANCY KATCRAFT, - - The landlady of the Atlantic House.
ELSIE, - - - - - - - - Her daughter.

NOTE.—The characters of Sammy and Fizzles can be doubled, and
the latter may be played with a dialect if desired.

TIME OF REPRESENTATION,—TWO HOURS AND A HALF.

SYNOPSIS OF INCIDENTS.

ACT I. THE HOME OF THE LIGHT-HOUSE KEEPER. An autumn
afternoon. The insult. True to herself. A fearless heart. The
unwelcome guest. Only a foundling. An abuse of confidence. The
new partner. The compact. The dead brought to life. Saved from
the wreck. Legal advice. Married for money. A golden chance.
The intercepted letter. A vision of wealth. The forgery. Within
an inch of his life. The rescue. TABLEAU.

ACT II. SCENE AS BEFORE; TIME, NIGHT. Dark clouds gather-
ing. Changing the jackets. Father and son. On duty. A struggle for fortune. Loved for himself. The halved greenbacks. The
agreement. An unhappy life. The detective's mistake. Arrested.
Mistaken identity. The likeness again. On the right track. The
accident. Will she be saved? Latour's bravery. A noble sacrifice.
The secret meeting. Another case of mistaken identity. The murder. Who did it? The torn cuff. "There stands the murderer!"
"It is false!" The wrong man murdered. Who was the victim?
TABLEAU.

ACT III. TWO DAYS LATER. Plot and counterplot. Gentleman and convict. The price of her life. Some new documents.
The halved bank-notes. Sunshine through the clouds. Prepared
for a watery grave. Deadly peril. Father and daughter. The rising tide. A life for a signature. True unto death. Saved! The
mystery solved. Denouement. TABLEAU.

COSTUMES.

ATWOOD. Grey suit, autumn overcoat, silk hat and patent leather shoes. Light hair, moustache and side-whiskers.

LATOUR. Dark suit, calf-skin shoes, derby hat. Black hair and beard, slightly tinged with grey.

GIGGLE. Fashionably dressed (à la dude), patent leather shoes, silk hat, etc. Jewelry, eye-glass and cane.

KATCRAFT. Dark trousers tucked in heavy boots, blue flannel shirt, soft slouch hat and pea-jacket. His hair is iron gray and he wears a grizzly beard.

HARLEY. Light trousers tucked in heavy boots, a neat blue flannel shirt, neck-tie, pea-jacket and derby hat. Black curly hair, but no beard.

MULLIN. In dress, build and appearance similar to LATOUR. An important factor of the play.

SAMMY. Dark trousers tucked in boots, flannel shirt, neck-tie and slouch hat. Light hair, but no beard.

FIZZLES. Dark navy blue suit and silk hat. Sandy hair and moustache.

MADELINE. Fashionably attired, wrap, parasol, etc. Blonde hair, exquisitely arranged.

ELSIE. Cambric polka-dotted dress, slippers, etc. Light hair, arranged in girlish fashion with a ribbon.

MRS. KATCRAFT. Matronly attire, dark dress, white apron, etc. Black hair, tastefully arranged, slightly tinged with grey.

PROPERTIES.

ACTS I and II. An old fashioned buffet, L. II., on which bottles, glasses, and decanters are arranged. Sofa R. H. Tables R. C. and L. C. Chairs R. and L. of tables. Easy chair near fireplace. Grate fire C. Screen, five feet high, before fire. Clock, writing materials and lamps, ready to light, R. and L., on mantel shelf at fireplace. Curtains at windows, looped back. Pocket-book containing banknotes, and pistol for ATWOOD. Pocket-book, letters and documents for LATOUR. Knives and pistols for KATCRAFT and MULLIN. Letter for SAMMY. Card for GIGGLE. Pencil for MULLIN. Tray, glasses and bottles ready at prompt stand. Basket. Crash (glass) ready for use. Matches on table, L. Handcuffs, pistol, and photograph for FIZZLES. Pipe and tobacco for LATOUR. Money for GIGGLE. Lighted cigarette for GIGGLE. Powder in paper for CLINCHER. Rain outside.

ACT III. Halved banknotes and documents in pocket-book, and pistol for ATWOOD. See that one of MULLIN's shoes is marked on the top "No. 17." Whistle and knife for KATCRAFT. Letter and warrant for FIZZLES. Memoranda and pencil for LATOUR. Letter (patched) for GIGGLE. Table and chairs R. C. Canvas cot up R. U. E. Lighted lamp, writing materials, jug of water and glass on table. Coils of rope piled up high, R. and L., above doors. Strong rope, an inch thick, for KATCRAFT. Nautical bric-a-brac arranged about stage.

STAGE SETTINGS.

ACTS I AND II.

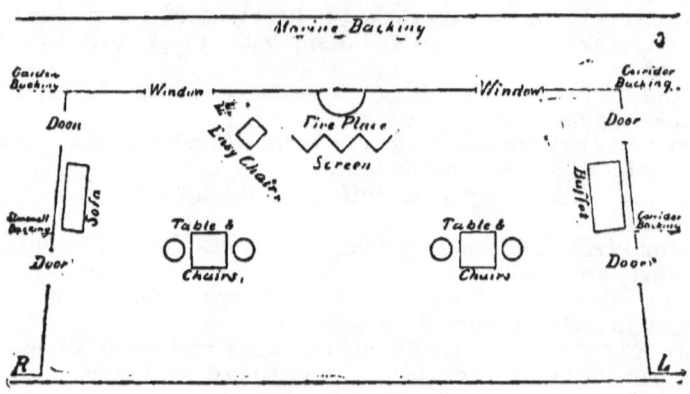

ACT III, SCENE 2.

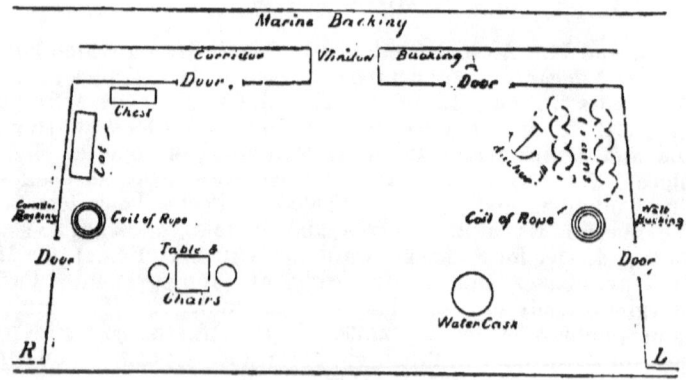

SCENE PLOT.

ACTS I and II.

Sitting-room in the Atlantic House at Barnegat. Plain chamber boxed in 4 G. Doors R. U. E. and L. U. E. Doors R. 2 E. and L. 2 E. (NOTE: Door R. 2 E. should open up stage, so as to screen GIGGLE at close of Act I.) Windows R. and L. at back. Mantel shelf and fireplace

C., at back, with grate fire. The scene is backed with a marine landscape which is seen through the windows R. and L. Backings at all entrances.

ACT III.

SCENE 1.—A landscape in 1st grooves.

SCENE 2.—Storage room on the ground floor of the light-house, boxed in 4 G. Doors R. C. and L. C., at back. Window C., in alcove. Doors R. 2 E. and L. 2 E. The scene is backed with a marine landscape which is seen through the window C. Moonlight effect on the backing, if practicable. Have suitable backings at all entrances.

STAGE DIRECTIONS.

The player is supposed to be facing the audience. R. means right; L., left; C., centre; R. C., right of centre; L. C., left of centre; D. F., door in the flat or scene running across the back of the stage; R. F., right side of the flat; L. F., left side of the flat; R. D., right door; L. D., left door; 1 E., first entrance; 2 E., second entrance; U. E., upper entrance; 1, 2 or 3 G., first, second or third grooves; up stage—toward the back; down stage—toward the footlights.

R.   R. C.   C.   L. C.   L.

SAVED FROM THE WRECK.

ACT I.

Scene: *Sitting room, neatly furnished, in the Atlantic House—Barnegat. Time, afternoon.*

As the curtain rises, ELSIE *is discovered waiving her handkerchief, while looking out of Window* R.

Enter ATWOOD R. U. E.

Atwood. (*On entering.*) Ah, good day, Miss Elsie. (*Coming down* C.) Was that one of your admirers, passed me just now?

Elsie. (*Down* R.) Yes, Squire—one of them.

Atw. I'll wager, I know one who has a better chance than he of winning you.

Elsie. Do you mean Harley?

Atw. (*Perplexed.*) Harley! Who is he?

Elsie. My father's assistant at the light-house.

Atw. Ah, yes, an ignorant boatman. You surely do not love such a booby?

Elsie. I don't know whether I love him, but one thing I *do* know; I don't like you, or any one else, who speaks ill of him.

Atw. Why, you surprise me, Miss Elsie! I always thought your ambition was of a higher plane. A young and pretty girl like you should have aspirations above this rookery of a place—and the love of a penniless boatman.

Elsie. And for what should I change it?

Atw. For the love of a man who would find you wealth, and change that cambric gown for one of silk, and cover those pretty fingers with diamonds.

Elsie. And who is the lover to do this?

Atw. (*Advancing to her.*) I.

6

Elsie. (*Retreating a step.*) You?

Atw. (*Business as before.*) Yes, I.

Elsie. (*Business as before.*) But you have a wife already.

Atw. True ; but I can at least make you my *protégée.*

Elsie. Pardon me, Squire ; in this old rookery, as you call it, I was born and reared, and taught by my mother to be an industrious and honest girl. If I prefer a cambric gown and the honest love of a penniless boatman to your diamonds, you must please score it to my ignorance. (*Xes L.*)

Enter HARLEY, R. U. E.

Atw. Listen ere it be too late, Elsie. If you wed the boatman your life will be one of poverty ; if you accept my protection, it will be one of luxury. Come, which shall it be?

Harley. (*Coming down C., unseen.*) Yes, which shall it be? The boatman's wife, or the Squire's *protégée?*

Elsie. (*Going to Harley.*) Why, the boatman's wife, Harley!

Atw. You've been eavesdropping, scoundrel! Were we equals, I should chastise you for this intrusion. (*Starts to go up stage, but is intercepted by* HARLEY.)

Har. A word with you, sir. Whatever there may be twixt our stations of life, remember, I come from a family that do not insult women. Go! (*Xes down R. in thought.*)

Atw. I trust, Miss Elsie, the next time I have the pleasure of a tête-a-tête with you, it will not be interrupted, especially by a nobody. Exit R. U. E.

Elsie. (L.) Harley! (*He takes no notice.*) Harley, dear——

Harl. (R.) Don't speak to me any more.

Elsie. Why not?

Harl. For encouraging that fellow.

Elsie. I don't encourage him, indeed I don't. (*Going to him.*) Harley, dear, you don't suppose I could prefer him to you?

Harl. I don't know.

Elsie. I am very sorry if I have offended you.

Harl. (*Turning round and kissing her.*) There! say no more about it.

Elsie. Why, Harley, your clothes are wet!

Harl. Yes, my dear, but I am none the worse for a little sea water.

Elsie. Unless it cools your love.

Harl. Ah! it would take all the water in the broad Atlantic to do that——

Elsie. (*Pointing to his clothes.*) But how did it happen?

Harl. As I was pulling homeward from the lighthouse, I noticed a boat drifting seaward, and in it was a lady—I went to her rescue, and——

Elsie. And you saved her?

Harl. Well, she'd have been drowned if I hadn't gone ; and—and—well, I have no wish to speak further on the subject.

Enter MRS. KATCRAFT L. U. E.

Mrs. Katcraft. (*Down C.*) Why, it's Harley! (*Kisses him.*) Well, I am so glad you have come home. Why, you are wet through !

Harl. Never mind, Mrs. Katcraft. A kiss from Elsie will keep the cold out.

Mrs. K. Now, Harley, don't you fill my girl's head with a lot of nonsense ; and above all, make no engagements. Remember you may yet find your parents.

Harl. Oh ! if you could assist me?——

Mrs. K. Ah, I know but little more than you ! When you were left in the charge of my husband about eighteen years ago, by a stranger who——

Enter CLINCHER KATCRAFT, R. U. E., *accompanied by Mullin, who remains up* C.

Clincher. (*Down L.*) Hello ! gossiping again ? (*To* MRS. KAT-CRAFT.) That tongue of yours is ever clanging--clanging, like the lighthouse bell when there's a fog.

Mrs. K. (*In a bitter tone.*) So, you have come home again?

Clinch. Yes ; and I'm going to stay home. Doubtless you'd as soon see the devil, as me.

Mrs. K. You read me aright, Clincher.

Clinch. And you call yourself a good wife. (*Looks at her a moment, then laughs.*) You must be madly in love with your husband--ha ! ha ! ha !--(*To Elsie.*) Come, bring me some whiskey.

Elsie. Yes, father.   Exit L. U. E.

Mrs. K. Speaking of wives, let me tell you, Clincher, I was a good and loving wife till I discovered, ah, too soon after we were married, the bitter bargain I had made.

Clinch. Ha! ha! discovered that I loved you, the landlady of the Atlantic House, for the sake of what you possessed.

Enter ELSIE *with two glasses and a bottle, and places them on table* R. C.

Elsie. (*Going to table.*) Your liquor, father.

Clinch. (*Tastes liquor.*) Hem! more water than spirit. (*Surveys* ELSIE.) Hem, you're growing pretty. Why, with your good looks, you ought to place yourself in the market for a swell.

Mrs. K. Clincher!

Clinch. Curse you, shut up; can't I give the girl some fatherly advice? Hereafter, keep a civil tongue or I'll teach you how to——

Mrs. K. By striking me?

Clinch. Yes, (*Raises hand.*) I'll do it.

Harl. (*Coming down* C. *between them.*) Strike her, Clincher Katcraft, and I will brain you.

Clinch. What! Young nobody's son—a foundling. I dare say your mother had good reasons for disposing of you——

Harl. Liar! (*About to strike him,* MRS. KATCRAFT *stays the blow.*)

Mrs. K. Hold, Harley! Go into the kitchen—leave him with me. Elsie; follow him. (*Accompanies them to door* L. U. E.) I cannot bear to see my child blush for her father. Go.

Exit HARLEY, L. U. E.

Elsie. (*At door.*) Mother!

Mrs. K. (*Kissing her.*) Have no fear, my darling.

Exit ELSIE, L. U. E.

Clinch. (*To* MRS. KATCRAFT.) Do you know, your sex is the strangest of the two?

Mrs. K. Do you remember the last time you raised your hand to me?

Clinch. Yes; and that boy was the cause of it. You wished to know too much.

Mrs. K. I knew he was left in your charge until his parents claimed him; that you were entrusted with large sums of money for his education. How have you carried out your promise? Have you not made a drudge—a slave of him? And when I asked you to do the boy justice, you struck me. That blow, Clincher Katcraft, killed every spark of love in my heart. I agreed, on condition you kept away from me, and took up your abode at the light-house, to give you every penny that I made at this business. Why, do you return to mar the quiet and peace of my life?

Clinch. Don't you think a man wishes to see his family now and then? My friend there, came down from New York to pay me a visit, and I thought I'd celebrate the event by having a couple of drinks here. Come, give us some liquor. Hurry up.

Mrs. K. Drinking the profits again. Much good may it do you.

Exit L. U. E.

Mullin. (*Advancing down* R. C.) If she were my wife, I'd soon break her in. (*Sits* R. *of table.*)

Clinch. (*Seated* L.) None of your interference in my domestic arrangements. This is better than Sing-Sing, eh?

Mul. Hush! If they find me I shall have to go back and finish my time.

Clinch. Now let us understand each other. I am tired of the light-house, with its long and weary days, its dark and silent nights.

Mul. You want to make money, don't you?

Clinch. Yes.

Mul. And so do I, and I'm not particular how I get it.

Clinch. I never was yet, and I ain't a going to be in my old age.

Enter GIGGLE, R. U. E.

Giggle. (*At* C. *up stage, looking* L.) Ah, here's a place for a sour mash. I revel in sour mashes; it's out of the common order of things. Ah, sour mash! Ha! ha! ha! (*Coming down stage* R. C. *laughing, not seeing* CLINCHER *and* MULLIN, *he strikes table with fist.*) It makes me laugh when I anticipate one.

Clinch. (*Rising.*) Who the deuce are you?

Gig. My name is Giggle—Augustus Giggle——

Mul. (*Aside as he rises.*) I thought I recognized him.

Gig. Ha! ha! ha! Funny name, isn't it? Giggle by name, and Giggle by nature. (*Pokes* KATCRAFT *in the ribs.*)

Mul. Why you'll hurt yourself laughing one of these days, Mr. Wriggle.

Gig. Not Wriggle! but Giggle—laughing is healthy. Ha! ha! ha! Why I was born laughing sir, and laughing I shall die. In fact to use an old expression, I shall die laughing—like the man who was tickled to death. Ha! ha! ha!

Clinch. Here, wife! wife! bring that liquor along.

Gig. Thanks awfully—I'll take a sour mash. Ha! ha! ha!

Clinch. Understand, you pay for your own drink.

Gig. Oh!—ha! ha! funny, very funny that.

Clinch. If you don't stop that giggling, I'll take you outside and give you a salt water ducking.

Gig. Funny man. Very good! Ha! ha! Excuse me—it's the way I have got—Ha! ha! ha!

Enter MRS. KATCRAFT, L. U. E. *with two glasses and bottle on tray.*

Clinch. (*Taking tray.*) Come into the next room, Mike. We don't wish to be disturbed with that laughing simpleton.

Exit *with Millin,* R. 2 E.

Gig. Excuse me—may I ask you two questions? Well, can I have a sour mash, and in which direction from here is Squire Atwood's house?

Mrs. Katcraft. You can have a sour mash with pleasure. Squire Atwood resides in the second villa, down the main road.

Gig. Madam, don't take me for an ordinary person or you'll be mistaken. I'm down here on business. I represent the firm— well a very firm firm, that's all. Ha! ha! ha!

Mrs. K. Bless the man! What is there to laugh at?

Gig. Nothing—positively nothing—that's why I laugh. Ha! ha! ha! I was about to remark, my firm is a lawyers'—and I am a clerk—no ordinary clerk, but a head one—like the coin that hadn't a tail on it. I visit Barnegat, Madam, merely to have a chat with Squire Atwood on important business.—Can I be accommodated with a bed beneath your celestial roost, and have an invigorating sour mash?

Mrs. K. Certainly, sir.

Gig. Thanks; bring me then the sour mash. Stay. (*Pointing to* R. 2. E.) Your best man in there?

Mrs. K. My best man? Well, he's my husband.

Gig. Ha! ha! I thought he was the head-light of this roost. Ha! ha! ha!

Mrs. K. What are you laughing at?

Gig. Ha! ha! I don't know, I never do—I laughed when I married.

Mrs. K. Oh, marriage is no laughing matter.

Gig. Just so, ha! ha! ha! It was to me. I laughed when my wife died. "Gussie," she said, "I am to be defunct." I took her feeble hand in mine. I stooped to take a parting kiss, and while the tears were rolling down my nose I laughed. Ha! ha! ha!

Mrs. K. And your wife.

Gig. Got up, broke my head with a poker, and then went to bed again and died.

Enter JOSEPH LATOUR, R. U. E.

Latour. (*Coming down* C.) This is the place. (*To* MRS. KATCRAFT.) Does Clincher Katcraft still keep this house?

Mrs. K. Yes, sir.

Lat. Can I have a room here to-night?

Mrs. K. Certainly, sir—I'll go at once and arrange it. Now if there's anything gives me pleasure, it is to make other people comfortable.   Exit L. U. E.

Gig. (*Seated* L. *of table* L.) A stranger in these parts?

Lat. (*Seated* R. *of table*.) Yes.

Gig. Your name?

Lat. Smith, if you like.

Gig. It doesn't suit; try another.

Lat. You are very curious, my friend.

Gig. Now, come, you don't really mean that.

Lat. Who are you?

Gig. A lawyer; don't be alarmed. I won't harm you. Ha! ha! ha! Will you have a sour mash with me?

Lat. No; you're a lawyer, eh?

Gig. Not a lawyer in full bloom, but a clerk in blossom. Managing clerk to the firm of Catchem and Fleesem, of Temple Court, New York, and down here on business.

Lat. I have just returned to America, and shall require a lawyer. Your card. (GIGGLE *gives him card which he puts into his pocket.*) My return to America is of a domestic nature. I am anxious to find a wife and child. Mine is a strange story, and you, being a lawyer, can perhaps be of service to me.

Gig. I'll not ask a retainer, if the narrative be romantic. I dote on romance, especially when it's spicy. Ha! ha! ha!

Lat. When I was about twenty years of age, I was a gentleman without fortune. I resolved to better my condition by a rich marriage. I met in this town a young lady supposed to be an heiress, she was handsome, and so I married her.

Gig. For her money. (CLINCHER *seen listening at* D. R. 2 E.)

Lat. Yes; but I had also spread abroad a rumor that I was rich. But we hadn't been married long before she discovered I was as poor as Job.

Gig. Ha! ha! ha!

Lat. And I found out that my supposed heiress was as poor as myself. At the expiration of a year, and after the birth of a child, we discovered our slender means exhausted. My wife proposed that we should separate to seek our fortunes in the world apart. Disgusted with her heartlessness—for in spite of my disappointment, I had learned to love—in a moment of angry passion, I deserted her, taking with me the child, whom I left here in charge of the landlord, with the last money I possessed in the world, but sufficient to maintain and educate him until I claimed him. I then took passage for Brazil, and, after eighteen years, have come home, a rich and prosperous man, to claim my son and find my wife.

Gig. To find your wife—what for?

Lat. Because I loved—still love her, and wish to make reparation for the grievous wrong I have committed.

Gig. And you have never heard from her?

Lat. Never! The ship in which I took passage was lost off Cape Hatteras. Every soul on board perished, I alone was *Saved from the Wreck!* (*Sees* CLINCHER; *rises; Xes to* C.) Why, you knave, you have been listening!

Clincher. I! No, no. I haven't heard a word.

Lat. (*Advancing to him.*) Clincher Katcraft, I've a few questions to ask you.

Clinch. (*Suppressed agitation.*) In a minute! Hello, Nancy—

wife—quick, I want you! (*Xing to* L. H. *as* MRS. KATCRAFT *enters* L. U. E.; *aside to her.*)   Quick! go and send that boy Harley to the light-house—to the devil.   Only get rid of him at once.

Mrs. K. I can't spare the time to look after him.

Clinch. Curse you, must I go myself?   Exit L. U. E.

Gig. Landlady, where is my sour mash?

Mrs. K. I've no lime juice in the house, sir; but there is plenty of it in the cellar.   (*To* CLINCHER *who re-enters* L. U. E.)   Will you go to the cellar for some lime juice?

Clinch. No, I won't.

Gig. I will bring it to you, and drink it for you, like the boy who took his brother' medicine for him.   Ha! ha! ha!

Mrs. K. Laughing again?

Gig. Why not?   I am contented and happy, and the more I laugh the merrier I become.   Ha! Mrs. Katcraft, I *do* enjoy myself.   Exit L. U. E., *followed by* MRS. KATCRAFT.

Clinch. (*Aside.*) I can't find that boy—I must get him out of the way—it won't answer my purpose for the father and son to meet yet, and find that I have misused the money.   (*To Latour.*) Now, sir, I am at your service.

Lat. So you have forgotten me, eh?

Clinch. You have the advantage of me.

Lat. Well, then I'll refresh your memory.

Clinch. (*Aside.*) I'm in for it, and will have to take his physic.

Lat. On the 18th of March, 1869, a child was left in your charge.

Clinch. I don't know nothing about it—This isn't a Foundling Asylum—and I ain't the keeper.

Lat. No! This is the Atlantic House at Barnegat, and you are Clincher Katcraft, its proprietor.   These little bits of paper (*Shows receipts.*) are your receipts, and engagement, to keep and educate the child till I should claim him.   Now, Clincher Katcraft —where is my son?

Clinch. I don't know—I ain't his shadow.

Lat. Beware! if you have not kept your word with me; if harm has come to him—what is he like?

Clinch. What's he like?   Well, he's like a fellow what's more trouble than he's worth—a good-for-nothing lazy cuss, what won't work, and won't speak the truth.

Lat. If this be true—bitter indeed has been my punishment. I ave lived but in the hope of clasping him to my heart—toiled ith but one desire to make him rich and happy—Clincher Katraft, you lie. Take me to him, let me judge for myself.

Clinch. He's at the light-house. You remain here to-night, and 1 the morning you will see him. (MULLIN *advances down* R., LINCHER *looking at him*.) Why, bless me! What a wonderful keness between you two men! You are as like as two peas, or s one pea that's been split in two. What will you drink, gentleien? (NOTE—MULLIN *and* LATOUR *should be similar in stature, 'ress and general appearance*.)

Lat. Nothing for me—(*Going towards* L. U. E.) I must write to 1y bankers for some money. If my son returns, let me know.

Exit L. U. E.

Clinch. I wonder if that boy has gone to the light-house—I don't ant him to meet his father yet. Exit L. U. E.

Mullin. Like me, eh! I wish I could have his money, and let im finish my time up the Hudson.—He is a rich man and I am n escaped convict. Exit R. U. E.

Enter GIGGLE *and* MRS. KATCRAFT, *with basket*, L. U. E.

Giggle. I repeat, Mrs. Katcraft, I must have lime juice in my ·hiskey.

Mrs. Katcraft. But we have none in the house.

Gig. Then the house must have some——

Mrs. K. Then it remains with you to go to the cellar and get it.

Gig. Give me the basket and I will go. (*Going towards* R. U. E.) Iere's a pretty how d'ye do; a fellow must wait on himself or go ·ithout his liquor. Ha! ha! ha!

Exit R. U. E.—(*Crash is heard off* R. U. E.)

Mrs. K. He's fallen on the broken bottles!

Enter ATWOOD *and* MADELINE, R. U. E.

Atwood. (L.) Now, madam, you have your wish.

Madeline. (C.) It is not often that I do.

Mrs. K. (*Offers chair*.) You will take a seat, Mrs. Atwood? It's roud and delighted I am to see you.

Mad. We have called for the purpose of thanking your son for his bravery.

Enter HARLEY and ELSIE, L. U. E.

Atw. And rewarding him.

Harley. Reward! I did not ask for a reward, sir; nor do I need it.

Atw. Ah, I'm afraid your pride o'er rides your station.

Mrs. K. Bless and prosperous us all, what has the boy been doing?

Mad. Saving my life, and at the risk of his own.

Elsie. Dear Harley!

Mad. We were out boating—but a sudden squall came and without our knowledge——

Atw. Madam, you forget yourself.

Mad. Perhaps; but I do not forget this young man who, seeing the danger, plunged into the surf, swam to our boat and brought us safe to land. It was the act of a brave and fearless man; but as he would not remain to receive my thanks, but hurried away as though ashamed of his own bravery, we sought him out to thank him.

Atw. And to pay him for his trouble. Here, young man, here are twenty dollars for the service you've rendered my wife.

Harl. Pardon me, Squire, but I can not accept it. I thank you sincerely, madam, but I only did what any *man* would have done under like circumstances.

Atw. You're too proud to accept the gift!

Harl. No, sir, only independent. (*Goes up* c.)

Enter CLINCHER, R. U. E.

Clincher. I say, wife, who left the cellar door open? I came nearly going through the opening. Ah, good evening all.

Atw. What do you think, Clincher; that son of yours refuses to accept a small gift from Mrs. Atwood for services rendered.

Mrs. K. His pride forbids his taking it. You can't blame the boy for that.

Clinch. Well, we are not so proud, sir—leastways I'm not. Give it to me, I'll take care of the gift for the boy until he grows to understand the value of presents.

Atw. Here, then. (*Gives him the money.*)

Clinch. (L.) Ha ! ha ! a crisp twenty dollar bill——

Harl. (*Advancing.*) Hold ! this is my affair. (*Taking money from* CLINCHER.) Squire, I can not, and will not accept your bounty. (*Returns him the bill.*)

Atw. Be it so.

Mad. Your son is a very proud young man.

Mrs. K. Bless you, madam, he's not my son.

Clinch. (*Aside.*) That woman's tongue is ever prattling. (*Aloud.*) He is an orphan whom we've brought up.

Atw. Out of charity, I presume?

Harl. Charity !

Clinch. (L. C.) Yes, sir ! My charity, and now he repays it by refusing the first opportunity of repaying me—ugh—I'm disgusted !

Mrs. K. (L. C.) 'Tis false—shame on you, Clincher, the truth goes the farthest—but, madam, you look fatigued ! Will you come into the dining-room and take a cup of tea? Exit CLINCHER, R. 2 E.

Mad. Thank you, I will. (*To* HARLEY.) Young man, you are a brave and noble fellow, and if ever you want a friend whose wealth and influence can assist you, come to me. Give me your arm.

Harl. With pleasure, madam.

Enter MULLIN, R. U. E.

Atw. (*To* MADELINE.) I expect some one from my lawyers; I'll walk to the house to see if he has come, and return with the carriage for you, my dear. *Au revoir.* Exit R. U. E.

Exeunt MADELINE, HARLEY *and* MRS. KATCRAFT, L. U. E. ELSIE *is following her when* MULLIN *stops her.*

Mul. Well, you are a pretty girl.

Elsie. Let me pass, if you please.

Mul. Don't be in a hurry, my dear. I'm a friend of your father's. In the parts we come from there are not many pretty girls.

Elsie. (*Trying to pass.*) I am wanted, sir—and——

Mul. Pay the toll then.

Elsie. The toll—what toll?

Mul. What toll! Why, a kiss—it costs you nothing—and it's a pleasure to me. (*Holds her in his arms.*)

Elsie. Release me!

Mul. Not without a kiss. (*Struggle.*)

Elsie. Harley! Harley!

Enter HARLEY, L. U. E.,—*turns and knocks* MULLIN *down* R., *as* CLINCHER *enters,* R. U. E.

Harley. I've a good mind to pitch you through that window (*Pointing to window* L. *at back.*) into the sea.

Clincher. What's the excitement all about?

Harl. Now, take my warning to heart. If you ever attempt to molest her again, I'll teach you a lesson to carry to your grave.

Exit, *with* ELSIE, L. U. E.

Clinch. (L. C.) What's the matter, Mullin?

Mul. (R.) Curse him, I'll make him pay for this.

Clinch. Come here, Mullin, sit down. (*They sit at table* L.) I want to avoid a reckoning with this Latour, and I have got a plan. You heard him tell his story?

Mul. Yes!

Clinch. He's returned a rich man. No one knows him in this country.

Mul. Go on.

Clinch. I can't get the idea out of my head, "Write to his bankers." Eh, Mike, do you know what I was saying to myself?

Mul. Not your prayers, I'll swear——

Clinch. No, partner. I was saying to myself that you are wonderfully like him. He ain't been seen for nearly twenty years, nobody remembers him. Now, if he was to die in the night—as we know all his history—how easy it would be for you to say as you was him, and——

Mul. To kill him and take his place, eh?

Clinch. That's it.

Enter SAMMY *with letter* L. 1 E., *runs against* CLINCHER *going up stage.*

Clinch. Hello, where are you going?

Sammy. To the post-office with this letter. (*Sees* MULLIN.) Why there's the gentleman that gave it me——

Mul. Yes ; I'll post it myself. (*Taking letter.*)

Clinch. I want you to go down to the beach and see whether my boat is fast, and remain out of doors, within calling distance, till I signal you.

Sam. Yes, sir. (*Going up* L. C.)   Exit, R. U. E.

Clinch. What's inside ?

Mul. I know a way to open it. Shall we ?

Clinch. Certainly.

Mul. (*Opens letter with pencil.*) It is a letter to his bankers, New York and Brazilian agents.

Clinch. I ain't no scholar ; what does it say ?

Mul. That he has arrived in America, and asks them to send him a check book—and that they'll know his signature by the enclosed letter. Ah, I see a way !

Clinch. So do I. Copy the letter and send your signature instead, eh ?

Mul. Yes, and when the check book comes draw the money. (CLINCHER *takes pen, ink and paper from mantel* C. *at back.*)

Clinch. Here's pen, ink and paper—quick ! Write it now. (MULLIN *writes letter, puts it into envelope ; seals it.*) But how about him ?

Mul. Get him into the light-house and keep him there till the money comes.

Clinch. Quick ! some one is coming.

Mul. (*Placing letter in* CLINCHER'S *hand.*) All right.

Enter LATOUR, L. U. E.

Latour. Has my son returned yet ?

Clinch. No, he's at the light-house ; but if you like, me and my partner will row you over there to see him—there's a good seaboat down on the beach.

Lat. Very well, come——

Clinch. In a minute.

Lat. I'll wait for you outside.   Exit, R. U. E.

Clinch. All right. He's walking towards death. (*Goes to window* R. *calls.*) Sammy ! Sammy ! (SAMMY *appears at window* R.) Post this letter for the gentleman. (SAMMY *takes letter and disappears.*)

Clinch. Now's your time ; he's waiting there, for us to take him to the light-house—he'll never be brought back again—the letter is posted—the game is in our hands.

Enter LATOUR, R. U. E.

Latour (*at* R. U. E.) Are you coming?
Clinch. Yes, yes.
Mul. Ha! ha! no one has seen him start.
Clinch. Ah, the game is ours!
Giggle. (*Unseen by them, with his clothes all torn and full of dust, appears with basket at* R. 2 E.) Not if I can prevent it. Ha! ha! ha!

Tableau.

MULLIN.	CLINCHER.	LATOUR.
R. C.	C.	L. U. E.

GIGGLE.
R. 2 E., behind door.

Curtain.

ACT II.

Scene: *Same as Act I. Time, Evening.* MRS. KATCRAFT *and* ELSIE *discovered with needlework, at table* R. C. MRS. KATCRAFT *seated* L., ELSIE *seated* R. HARLEY *at grate-fire,* C. *at back, drying jacket; he takes* CLINCHER'S *jacket from off chair, which is drying before fire and puts it on. Music, " The little ones at Home," plaintively played at rise of curtain.*

Mrs. Katcraft. You are not looking well, Elsie! What's the matter?
Elsie. Merely a nervous headache, mamma. Caused, no doubt, by the excitement of Harley's quarrel with Squire Atwood.

Enter CLINCHER, R. U. E.

Clincher. Curse that fellow Giggle, he's prevented our little game. He has stopped Latour from going to the light-house. I must prevent father and son from meeting. (*Sees* HARLEY *at fire.*) Hello! It's time you were at the light-house.

Harley. (*Putting* CLINCHER'S *jacket on.*) I'm off. I have borrowed your jacket.

Clinch. Ugh!

Harl. Good night, Mrs. Katcraft.

Mrs. K. Good night, Harley.

Harl. Good night, Elsie. (*Aside to her.*) After the house is closed I'll put off from the light-house. At the usual signal, come down to me at the window, there. (*Pointing to window* L.)

Clinch. (*Goes to chair near fire, takes* HARLEY'S *jacket.*) Why, it's dry enough already, it's warmer than mine—I'll wear it.

Elsie. Yes, you may expect me, Harley. (*Gives* HARLEY *kiss, and* Exits, *with* MRS. KATCRAFT, L. 2 E.)

Clinch. Come, break away. I hate such immorality. (*Aside.*) If he doesn't hasten, they'll meet. Come along, Harley.

Harl. (*Going towards* R. U. E.) I'm ready.

Enter LATOUR, R. U. E.

Clinch. Curse the luck——

Latour. (*At* R. U. E.) Who is this?

Harl. You know well enough who I am.

Lat. Harley, the adopted son of Clincher Katcraft, eh?

Harl. I am.

Clinch. (*Aside.*) Ha! ha! ha! He has mistaken him for Mike Mullin.

Lat. Ah! then I have arrived in time.

Harl. Aye, to be thrown from that window (*Pointing to window* R. *at back,*) if you are not careful.

Lat. Young man, you are insolent.

Harl. Insolent! so were you to Elsie. Who and what are you—some jail-bird, no doubt.

Lat. (*Advancing down* R. C., *aside.*) Clincher then was right, and this violence proves him unworthy of my love. (*Turning and going up to* HARLEY.) Young man, I have travelled thousands of miles to meet you—to take you by the hand—to lift you from your humble calling and bring you prosperity and fortune. My expectations have not been realized. In you I thought to find

a noble-hearted lad, but instead I meet a quarrelsome and violent
rowdy—I cannot express how grieved I am—(*About to go to* R. U.
E., *but is intercepted by* HARLEY.)   Fare-well, and forever.

Harl. (*Intercepting him.*) Stay! Do you come from my father?

Lat. Yes.

Harl. Then if he is like you, tell him from me I do not seek his
fortune, nor his aid. He left me helpless among strangers, to be
fed and clothed on charity, to grow without education like a weed
in the field.

Lat. Left you helpless! It is false! Poor and friendless, he
was compelled to leave America, and you in the charge of
strangers. He left 3000 dollars with your guardian and every
year remitted other sums.

Clinch. (*Aside.*) It's getting too warm for me. I'm off.

Exit, L. U. E.

Lat. Away—abroad, among constant danger and disease—
where every day he held his life in his hands, he dared not send
for you—but you were always in his thoughts. He toiled and
fought for fortune with one desire, to come back home to take you
to his heart.

Harl. Can this be true?

Lat. Demand the truth from Clincher Katcraft, and then learn
what you have lost by insulting me.

Harl. Insulting you! a ruffian who had the cowardice to molest
a helpless girl.

Lat. I—never.

Enter MULLIN, R. U. E., *unseen; he goes to fire* C.

Harl. Are you not the drunken ruffian who insulted Elsie Katcraft?

Lat. No! there must be some mistake. (*Suddenly.*) Ah! the
man like me, Katcraft's companion! (*Sees* MULLIN.) There—
there is the man you mean.

Harl. (*After comparing both men.*) I have been deceived by the
likeness. I ask your pardon. I mistook you for that man. (*Pointing to* MULLIN.) Believe me, I am not unworthy of your love. I
—oh!—sir, forgive me.

Lat. (*Holding out his hand.*) My son!

Harl. My father!

Lat. I have much to tell you and explain.

Harl. But my duty at the light-house has commenced.

Lat. I'll walk down with you. Henceforth, Harley, we will face the world together.

Harl. Father!

Lat. My boy! (*Places arm round* HARLEY'S *shoulders, and* Exeunt *together*, R. U. E., *as* CLINCHER *enters* L. U. E. *He comes down and sits* R. *of table* L.)

Clinch. I tell you, Mullin, I'm off the job.

Mul. Well, all right. Had it not been for that laughing hyena, I'd soon settle him.

Enter GIGGLE, R. U. E.

Giggle. Ha! ha! ha! but the fool won't be settled. (*Coming down, sits* L. *of table* L., CLINCHER *rises, and goes up* C. *to fire;* MULLIN *crossing to table* L., *takes seat just occupied by* CLINCHER.

Mul. Now, Mr. Sniggle——

Gig. Giggle! not Sniggle, and Giggle has a tale to tell.

Mul. A tale to tell, eh? I can tell a tale too, Mr. Figgle. (*Sitting* R. *of table.*)

Gig. Giggle, not Figgle.

Mul. You seem to have a bad memory for faces. I'll refresh you.

Gig. Refresh me, ha! ha! ha! mine will be sour mash.

Mul. Did you ever hear of the firm of Large, Sales and Profits?

Gig. Ah! (*Starts.*)

Mul. Oh, I see you have. My tale is of two clerks employed there some five years ago. Chapter the first.—One of these clerks was fond of betting, and one was fond of laughing, but both of them wanted money. Chapter the second.—A check was forged, written by the betting clerk and presented by the laughing clerk. (*Giggle starts and is dazed for the moment, then laughs.*)

Gig. Ha! ha! ha!

Mul. The forgery was discovered, and one morning the two unfortunate clerks found themselves under arrest. Chapter the third. —One of the clerks was found guilty and sentenced; but the other for the want of evidence, was discharged. Chapter the fourth.— I am the convicted clerk, and you are the discharged one.

Gig. Ha! ha! ha! A very funny story.

Mul. But you don't laugh quite so heartily as you did. Now I have come down in the world and you have gone up. You are head clerk in a very respectable firm, who, if they know your past antecedents, would dismiss you from their service.

Gig. But I—was exonerated——

Mul. On the contrary—you were discharged. The evidence was insufficient then, but I could now produce that which would convict you, even at this late day.

Clinch. Why don't you laugh now, Mr. Giggle. (*Giggle looks serious;* MULLIN *and* CLINCHER *laugh at him.*)

Gig. (*Forced laugh.*) Laugh! ha! ha! ha! I can always laugh. Ha! ha! ha! (*Rising, goes down stage* R.)

Mul. Now, Mr. Giggle, mind your own business and I'll mind mine. Interfere again in my affairs and I will expose you. Silence for silence.—(*Seeing* MRS. KATCRAFT *who enters* L. U. E.) Remember!   **Exit,** *with* CLINCHER, L. U. E.

Gig. (*In thought.*) After these years, the only shadow on my life comes up. It's funny, ha! ha! ha! what he says is true enough. I was innocent—what of that? If the firm knew of my disgrace I should be discharged.

Mrs. Katcraft. (*Coming down* C.) What's the matter? You look dull, Mr. Piggle.

Gig. Giggle! not Piggle—Dull! I'm as happy as a bird in Spring—ha! ha! ha! Let's have a sour mash.

Mrs. K. Yes.

Gig. Don't spare the lemon, Mrs. Katcraft—ah! by the by—make a pint of it while you're at it——

(*Sings.*)   "When you're sad and lack dash,

       Take a strong sour mash,

       It drives away sorrow and care——"

Ah! Mrs. Katcraft, the fellow who first compounded that tonic was a genius. Ha! ha! ha!

     Enter DETECTIVE FIZZLES, R. U. E.

Fizzles. (R.) Are you Mrs. Katcraft?

Mrs. K. (*Serving* GIGGLE *from buffet*, L. H.) That's my name.

Gig. Ha! ha! ha! Mrs. Katcraft, you know when to put liquors on the buffet—when night's drawing on, to save steps—

       Exit L. 2 E., *with glass, singing*

       "When you're sad and lack dash, etc."

Fiz. Are you the wife of Clincher Katcraft, keeper of the light-house here at Barnegat?

Mrs. K. Yes, sir.

Fiz. Have you any stranger stopping in the house?

Mrs. K. Yes, sir.

Fiz. Of suspicious appearance?

Mrs. K. Yes, sir. Very suspicious.

Fiz. Where is he?

Mrs. K. Somewhere about the house.

Enter LATOUR, R. U. E.

(MRS. KATCRAFT, *Pointing to* LATOUR.) Ah, there he is!

Latour. (*at* R. U. E.) What could have been the meaning of the warning not to go to the light-house till I had seen Giggle? I'll wait and do so. (*Coming forward.*)

Fiz. (*Aside to* MRS. KATCRAFT.) The man corresponds with this photo to a dot. (*Aloud.*) How do you do?

(MRS. KATCRAFT *retires* U P C., *and* Exits, L. U. E.)

Lat. How do you do?

Fiz. What's your name, eh?

Lat. That's my business. What's yours?

Fiz. That's my business. It's no good, I know you. Michel Mullin, you're my prisoner.

Lat. You are mistaken, officer.

Fiz. Officer! I am a detective.

Lat. (*Filling pipe.*) Have you a match?

Fiz. No, sir.

Lat. (*Taking match from table* L., *and lighting pipe.*) I thought not. (FIZZLES *places handcuffs on* LATOUR'S *wrists while the latter is lighting pipe.*)

Fiz. These will match you though.

Lat. You're awfully clever. Have you that trick patented or is it one of Uncle Sam's?

Fiz. Well, you're a cool one.

Lat. Brought about by the climate. Just feel in my right hand inside coat pocket. That's it. Take out the contents. (FIZZLES *opens and reads papers as* LATOUR *describes them.*) Receipt for passage by ship " Sovereign of the Sea," from Rio Janeiro to New York, Joseph Latour, mining engineer.

Fiz. Right.

Lat. Receipt for baggage belonging to Joseph Latour, left at the Claredon Hotel. (*Fizzles takes up another package and examines it.*) Letters and documents of various kinds—bankers' drafts, etc.,—Joseph Latour.

Fiz. Right.

Lat. Will you kindly take back these pieces of jewelry?

Fiz. I have made a mistake. (*Releasing him.*) I beg your pardon.

Lat. Thank you. (*Relights pipe.*)

Fiz. You're wonderfully like Michel Mullin, the man I am after. But never mind, I'll have him yet. Exit, R. U. E.

Lat. He must be the man Clincher said resembled me. Shall I put this detective on his track? No, poor devil, I'll give him a chance. Exit, L. 2 E.

Enter ATWOOD *and* GIGGLE, R. U. E.

Atwood. (*Coming down,* L. C.) Really, Mr. Giggle, I see nothing to laugh at.

Giggle. Don't you? That's funny. Ha! ha! ha! No more do I.

Atw. Mr. Giggle! Will you, on behalf of your firm, advance me this money?

Gig. I am afraid I can't. (*Producing money.*) Here is the $2,500 the firm promised. But as regards more, like the man who was asked to hang himself, they would rather not.

Atw. My wife has plenty of money, or rather say property.

Gig. Which she will not consent to have mortgaged—Sensible woman; ha! ha! ha! Why, Squire, it's like the mummy in the museum; you mustn't touch. Ha! ha! ha!

Atw. At her death, it comes to me.

Gig. If she does'nt leave it to some one else. Don't fear, she isn't going to die so soon. Folks are not so obliging as that now-a-days—Ha! ha! ha! If I stay much longer here, I'll explode, like the man who took a lighted candle to see where the gas escaped. Exit, R. U. E.

Atw. (*Alone.*) What is to be done? I must have money. Oh, if my wife were to die!

Mrs. Katcraft. (*Outside* L. U. E.) I'm glad, Mrs. Atwood, the rest has done you good—(Enter MRS. KATCRAFT *and* MADELINE, L. U. E.) Now, while you remain here, I will make you a hot cup of tea.

Madeline. Do so, if you please—(*Coming down* C.)

Mrs. K. I'll prepare it instantly. Oh, I do enjoy making every body comfortable. Exit, L. U. E.

Atw. (*Advancing to* MADELINE.) My dear! (MADELINE *pays no attention to him, Xes to chair* R., *and sits.*) One word, my dear——

Mad. You are unusually polite, Squire.

Atw. Are you not my wife?

Mad. I am but too bitterly aware of it.

Atw. Remember, you have but to comply with my wishes——

Mad. And turn over my fortune to you, to squander as you did your own? Ah, no! when your father vested me with a dowry, he was well aware of your true character. He had no desire to see his son's wife one day or other without home or fortune.

Atw. You know I am embarrassed. Why desire to keep it?

Mad. I have reasons of my own

Atw. Remember, at your death it goes to your husband.

Mad. And you must wait till then. (*Rises.*)

Enter MRS. KATCRAFT, L. 3 E.

Mrs. Katcraft. The tea is quite ready.

(MADELINE *goes towards* L. U. E; *but is intercepted by* ATWOOD.)

Atw. The carriage is here. Will you not ride home, Madeline?

Mad. Thank you, no—at least not at present. Exit, L. U. E.

Mrs. K. How polite! What a happy couple they must be. Exit, L. U. E.

Atw. At her death! Oh, if the devil would but place the means within my grasp! (*Retires up stage* C.)

Enter CLINCHER *and* MULLIN, R. U. E.

Clincher. Honesty—ha! ha! ha!—My notion of honesty is keeping out of prison.

Atw. Mind you do keep out.

Clinch. (*Surprised.*)   Phew! the Squire!

Atw. Who is this with you?

Clinch. A friend.

Atw. (*Looking at* MULLIN.)   Um! answers the detective's description, and like the portrait. Ah, how do you do, Michael Mullin—(*Xing to him.*)

Mullin. Eh! that ain't my name.

Atw. No, of course not; that's why you turned pale. Returning to Sing-Sing is even worse than the light-house—oh, come, I know you.

Mul. Curse you, I'll—(*Draws knife—*CLINCHER *stops him.*)

Atw. Keep quiet and listen to me. I can speak freely to you both, because you are both in my power.

Clinch. (R.)   How?

Atw. Because you, Clincher Katkraft, keep stolen and smuggled property at the light-house; and you (*To* MULLIN.) are an escaped convict.

Clinch.
Mul.   } (R.)   Ah!

Atw. As you entered, you saw a carriage at the door?

Clinch. Yes, your wife's.

Atw. (L.)   It will have to cross the bridge over the creek. Is that bridge safe?

Clinch. (C.)   You know it ain't—why, if it wasn't for one particular support that I knows of, when the carriage crossed the person inside would——

Atw. Be killed, eh?

Clinch. Yes.

Atw. Well, if an accident should happen to that bridge to-night——

Clinch.
Mul.   } Well!—

Atw. I'd give $500 to some deserving charity.

Clinch. We are that deserving charity. (*To* MULLIN.)   What do you say, partner? It can be done without risk.

Mul. I say—do it.

Clinch. How is the money to be paid?

Atw. After the accident, or you might forget to do it.

Clinch. No; before the accident, or *you might forget to pay*.

Atw. (*Selecting from wallet five $100 notes.*) Well! here are five one hundred dollar bills. We'll cut them in halves—each half being useless without its mate. You shall keep these (*Gives them half notes*), and I'll keep these. Now, after the accident, you can have these halves.

Clinch. That will do. (*To* MULLIN.) Here, let's divide. (*Gives* MULLIN *two and a half of the notes.*)

Mul. (*Looking around, sees* FIZZLES *at Window* L.) Ah! look out, we are watched. I'm off. (*Drops bills, rushes to* L. 2 E., *and stumbles against* LATOUR, *who enters;* FIZZLES *disappears;* CLINCHER *and* ATWOOD *look out of window,* L.)

Latour. (*To* MULLIN.) Mind where you are running!

Mul. I'm in a hurry.

Exit, MULLIN, L. 2 E. LATOUR *sits on chair near fire,* C.

Atw. I cannot see anyone—(*Taking head in from window.*)

Clinch. Perhaps he's gone round to the back of the house.

Fizzles. (**Enters** L. 2 E., *looking back.*) Was it he that I passed? (*Sees* LATOUR.) No! He is here! (*Advancing to* LATOUR.)

Lat. Here's who? Do you want to put those bracelets on me again?

Fiz. Tricked again, confound it!   Exit, R. U. E.

Atw. You must be mistaken, Clincher. (*Advancing down* C.) Here is your share of the bills. (*Picking up bills dropped by* MULLIN ; *giving them to* LATOUR, *whom he mistakes for the former.*)

Clinch. Come along. The bridge will break, the carriage will fall and, oh! if I could only get my wife into it.

Exit ATWOOD, L. U. E.

Enter MULLIN, R. U. E., *coming towards* CLINCHER.

Clinch. Come along, Mullin. (*Going towards* R. 2 E.)

Mullin. (*Partly aside.*) Doubled him again.

Clinch. Are you coming, Mullin, or do you intend standing there all night?

Mul. (*Following him.*) You needn't shout in that fashion, Clincher. I'm coming.   Exit, *with* CLINCHER, R. 2 E.

Lat. (*At fire.*) What's this accident? Loosen the supports and get rid of his wife! Can it be, that they are planning a murder under the disguise of an accident? (*Examines notes.*) Two halves and a quarter of three $100 bills, eh! I'll see what this means. (*Rises.*)

Enter MADELINE *and* MRS. KATCRAFT, L. U. E.

Madeline. (*Coming to* C.) I am much obliged to you for your attention.

Mrs. Katcraft. I hope, madam, we shall be honored by your presence more often.

Mad. That you will, Mrs. Katcraft. (Enter ATWOOD, L. U. E.) I'm prepared to return home, Squire. Is the carriage ready?

Atw. (L.) Yes, my dear; (*Aside.*) ready to carry you to your death. Shall I spare her? I'll give her another chance. (*Aloud.*) A word my dear ; will you let me have the money?

Mad. Not while I live, Squire.

Atw. (*Aside.*) Then let my plans do their worst. Madam, I await you. (*Bowing to* MADELINE.)

Mad. (*To* MRS. KATCRAFT.) Till we meet again, adieu.

Exit *with* ATWOOD, R. U. E., *after* MRS. KATCRAFT *has opened door; she follows off.*

Lat. (*Coming down* C.) My wife !

Gig. (*Who enters* R. U. E.) What !

Lat. Where is she going?

Gig. To her carriage, to drive home.

Lat. Ha! which way?

Gig. The nearest way, of course, across the bridge.

Lat. Great heavens! I see it all ; she is to be the victim. There is no time to be lost. (*Going up* C. *rapidly to* R. U. E.)

Gig. Where are you going?

Lat. To prevent a crime !   Exit, R. U. E.

Gig. (*Sitting at table*, R.) His wife ! Oh, here's a how dye do! a pretty how dye do! Ha! ha! ha! (Enter ATWOOD, R. 2 E., *and Xes to* L.) How would you like to lose your wife, sir, and her fortune, too?

Atwood. Her fortune ! Ah, no! If I lose my wife, I gain a fortune.

Gig. Oh, no, you wouldn't.

Atw. Oh, yes, I should. At her death her fortune reverts to her husband.

Gig. But you are not her husband.

Atw. Not her husband! Then who is?

Gig. Who? Ha! ha! ha! Why, Joseph Latour.

Atw. Ah! impossible. I was legally married to her.

Gig. So was he; only he was married first, ha! ha! ha!

Atw. Idiot!

Gig. She was married before—had a row—husband went to sea —supposed to be drowned—was *saved from the wreck*—married you—came into a fortune from your father, at his death, after her marriage with you—husband now turns up, and you are nowhere —like the man in the balloon that never came down again. Oh, Squire Atwood, if I don't laugh, I shall burst like the man who swallowed the bombshell.

Atw. (*Aside.*) If this be true, I am lost indeed! (*As he rushes to door*, R. U. E., *crash is heard, like the breaking of timbers, followed by a scream.*) Too late! (*Giggle laughs*; MULLIN enters R. U. E.) Ah! the bridge?

Mullin. (*Coming down* C.) Broken down. (*Taps Giggle on shoulder; he looks round, sees* MULLIN, *and immediately stops laughing.*)

Gig. I'll make myself scarce.   Exit, R. 2 E.

Atw. But the carriage!

Mul. Is smashed to pieces.

Atw. And my wife?

Enter LATOUR, R. U. E., *carrying* MADELINE, *fainting*.

Latour. (*Placing* MADELINE *in chair near screen.*) Is safe, Squire Atwood.

Mul. (*Aside to* ATWOOD.) Curse it! All our work for nothing! I must see, Clincher.   Exit, R. 2 E.

Enter MRS. KATCRAFT, L. U. E.

Mrs. Katcraft. Bless and preserve us, what has happened?

Lat. Something was wrong with the bridge. I was hastening to overtake the carriage, and had just reached the side—the horses' feet were on the bridge—when I seized the lady and dragged her out as the bridge, the horses, and the carriage sank below.

Mrs. K. (*Attending* MADELINE.) An accident!

Lat. (R.) Or an attempted murder, eh, Squire?

Madeline. (*Reviving.*) What is this?—Where am I? And where is he who saved me? (*Sees* LATOUR.) Ah, living—Oh! my brain is wandering.

Lat. (*To* MRS. KATCRAFT.) Quick! some water.

Mrs. K. (*At back of chair.*) Bless and preserve us, yes. (*Xes to buffet, pours water into glass and gives it to* LATOUR.)

Mad. (C. *at back.*) Am I dreaming—no—no, you were lost off Cape Hatteras—I—oh—impossible! The memories of twenty years return—my husband!—my husband!

Atw. (*Advancing to her.*) Your husband is here, madam.

Mad. (*With a shudder.*) No, no, not you! The child that was taken from me, where—where is he?

Atw. (L. C.) The child! (*Takes glass of water from* MRS. KATCRAFT.) I will give it to her. Leave us, Mrs. Katcraft.

Mrs. K. If you wish it—yes, sir—(*Goes to* LATOUR, R.)

Atw. (L.) Here, take this, madam. (*Offering glass of water.*)

Mad. No, no, I——

Lat. (*Going* R. *towards* MADELINE.) Permit me.

Atw. Excuse me—this lady is my wife.

Lat. Are you sure of that?

Atw. Arise, madam, and follow me.

Mad. No, no, I cannot--the shock—I——

Atw. Madame, I have discovered your secret—that when you married me you had a husband living.

Mad. I believed he was dead.

Atw. But you did not tell me that you had a child. I have heard this husband say it is alive—but let him beware before he claims you as his wife.

Lat. (*Who has been in conversation with* MRS. KATCRAFT, *quickly turns to him.*) Beware, and why?

Atw. (*To* MADELINE.) Because, I'll send you to a prison.

Mad. A prison!

Atw. Aye! to a prison for bigamy. Let this husband but avow himself, and I shall charge you. How will you like to stand your trial in a criminal's dock, and receive a felon's sentence.

Lat. You dare not do it.

Atw. Dare not! The hour this husband comes to claim his wife, makes her a felon.

Mad. Squire, you are a coward.

Atw. A coward!

Mad. Aye, a coward, or you would not persecute a woman. I confess my previous marriage. My husband, in a fit of frenzy and angry passion, misunderstood and deserted me, and took with him our child. Heaven knows how, in my heart, I mourned his loss. He was wrecked off Cape Hatteras, and as I believed, was drowned. Thus I was left a childless widow, without a friend or protector, defenceless in the world. Unknown to myself a fortune had been left me by your father, who, it seems, was largely indebted to my father, for monetary loans advanced years ago. And you married me. It is true, I did not tell you my secret, for it was a sorrow sacred to myself. But my husband, let him but speak the word, and come what may, I will own him before the world. You, I defy! Now do your worst!

Atw. Curse you! (*Raises his arm to strike her.* MADELINE *screams and swoons.*)

Lat. Stand back! Raise but your arm again, and I will strike you to my feet.

Atw. You! Ha! ha! And who are you?

Lat. I am—ah! (*Aside.*) No, no, I can not disgrace, dishonor——(*Xes* L.)

Mrs. K. (*Near her.*) Poor lady! she has swooned!

Atw. Rise, madam, and come with me.

Mrs. K. No, sir! Nancy Katcraft is mistress in this house; she shall stay with me. (*Leads her to* L. U. E., MADELINE, *as she goes, turns and looks affectionately at* LATOUR.)

Mad. Joseph!

Lat. (*Going to her.*) Madeline! have courage—

   Exeunt MRS. KATCRAFT *and* MADELINE, L. U. E.

(*Turning to* ATWOOD.) I shall do nothing to bring dishonor upon her name. I will go away, but I will not leave her to your mercy, to be murdered.

Atw. Murdered!

Lat. (*Coming toward* ATWOOD.) Aye, murdered! I overheard your plot, and know that you had sent a helpless woman to her death.

Atw. 'Tis false! You have no proof.

Lat. But I have. These half bank-notes. (*Shows bank-notes.*) Now, Squire Atwood, we can deal on equal terms.

Atw. (*Aside.*) Trapped! I must see Clincher, and at once. I have a bold and desperate game to play. (*Falls into thought.*)

Lat. Squire Atwood! Come, what is your reply? That woman shall never cross your threshold again. (*Seeing* MULLIN, *who enters* R. U. E.) But this is neither the time nor place to settle our accounts. (*Xing to* R.)

Atw. Be it so—to-morrow.

Lat. Aye! to-morrow.

Atw. (*Aside to* MULLIN.) Where's Clincher?

Mullin. Down by the shore.

Atw. (*Aside.*) I must strike a desperate blow to-night. Good ; to-morrow—he may not live to see the morrow.   **Exit, R. 2 E.**

Lat. (*Goes to table* R.; *sits* L.) What can be done, and how can I save her from disgrace? I must have time to think.

Mul. (*Seated* R. *of table.*) You don't seem in very good spirits.

Lat. Do you think so?

Mul. I want to speak to you, Mr. Latour.

Mrs. Katcraft. (*Who enters* L. U. E.) Poor lady! She is ill indeed. I have called Elsie to attend to her. She shall sleep in her bed to-night.   **Exit, R. U. E.**

Mul. It seems strange that people should say that you and I are so much alike; they might make a mistake.

Lat. How do you mean?

Mul. Well, for instance, if anything happened to you what is to prevent me saying I were you.

Lat. Proofs my friend. I carry upon my person, at all times, documents that would prove who I am. (*Producing package of letters from coat pocket.*) There, they are. (*Replaces them.*)

Mul. (*Aside.*) It's all right. I must have those papers.

Lat. Thus far, those papers have proved invaluable. I would have been taken to Sing-Sing to finish your time were it not for them.

Mul. Eh! What do you mean?

Lat. Nothing much, only a detective has been here and mistaken me for you.

Mul. Ah!

Lat. Don't be alarmed. I said nothing to betray you.

Enter GIGGLE *and* MRS. KATCRAFT, R. U. E.

Giggle. (*Smoking cigarette.*)   Mrs. Katcraft, is my bed ready?

Mrs. Katcraft. Of course it is.

Gig. Then I will prepare to take possession of it.   Now, my dear Mrs. Katcraft, there's another thing of as great importance; my sour mash.   I must have a soothing tonic, as the baby says who wants his paregoric.   You will prepare an extra quantity— say a half-pint and leave it on your quaint buffet.   (*Pointing to buffet.*) Should I crave in the night for a drink, I can have it without disturbing any one.   (*Goes to table* L., *sits* R. H., *and takes his shoes off.*)

Mul. (R. *at table.*)   Will you have a drink?

Lat. (*Rising.*)   No! I'll go to bed.   I have suffered one deep and bitter disappointment, and had best prepare myself for an- other.   If it should be as Clincher Katcraft says, and this boy is really unworthy, better, far better, to have gone down on the "Sovereign of the Sea" off Cape Hatteras.

Mrs. K. Your room sir, is the third one, this way along the hall.

(Pointing L. U. E.)

Lat. Thank you.   Good-night.   Exit, L. U. E.

Gig. Mrs. Katcraft, give me a sour mash, a sort of a night cap. (MRS. KATCRAFT *goes to buffet;* GIGGLE *sees her, arranging drink, which she brings to him.*) Ah, I see you anticipated my previous remark, and prepared the liquor in advance.

Mrs. K. The amount already drunk by you, gave the thought. I had no wish to be aroused at night, only to hear you calling aloud for a sour mash.

Gig. Wonderful head, ha! ha! ha! You can't have too much of a good thing—like the lady who had twins twice running. Ha! ha! ha! h—(*Suddenly stops, as* MULLIN *looks at him.*) I shall really get drunk if I don't let up on sour mashes. (*Slowly his head falls on table—the stupor from liquor is quite perceptible in him.*)

Enter CLINCHER, R. U. E.

Clincher. (*Aside.*)   The Squire has offered me double the money to put this Latour out of his way.   Shall I take Mullin or do the job on my own account? (*Sees* MRS. KATCRAFT *near fire, watch- ing him.*) Hullo! wife—where is Mr. Latour?

Mrs. K. Just this minute gone to bed.   He seemed low-spirited,

poor gentleman. I intend to take him some brandy ; it may help
to cheer him a bit—at least it will assist him to sleep easy.

Clinch. Prepare it right away ; I'll take it to him. (*Aside.*)
I've got a drug. I'll slip it into the liquor and make him sleep
the slumber from which there's no waking.

Mrs. K. (*Who has prepared drink at buffet.*) There's a toddy
that will soothe his feelings, I'll be bound, (*Going up stage.*)

Clinch. Hurry up—give it to me. (*Taking glass—aside.*) This
will do its duty. (*Slips powder into glass* and Exit L. U. E. MRS.
KATCRAFT *fastens door* R. U. E., *and arranges the place for the
night.*)

Mul. (*Seated* L.) Why should I take Clincher in the swim—
why not have the game all to myself? He's drugged that liquor.
I could get into the house later on—when they are all in bed—get
his clothes and that precious packet and pocket book. The game
is in my hands. (*Rain heard without, which continues till end of
act.*)

Enter CLINCHER, L. U. E.

Mrs. K. Clincher, I've fastened up the place for the night, ex-
cept the side door (*Pointing to* D. L. 2 E.) I'll leave you to fasten
that when these gentlemen (*Pointing to* MULLIN *and* GIGGLE)
retire, or go. Good night. Exit, L. U. E.

Clinch. ⎫
Mul. ⎬ Good night.

Mul. (*Rises.*) I'm off.

Clinch. What, ain't you going to remain here to-night?

Mul. No! I'm off the job anyhow to-night. I'm going. Open
the door and let me out.

Clinch. Oh! if that's your style, all right. (*Opens door*, R. U. E.)
There, and glad to get rid of you.

Mul. The same to you—and go to the devil.

Exit, R. U. E.

Clinch. I wonder what his game is ; had he drunk too much, or
was he only shamming? No matter, he's gone, and it's all the
better. (MULLIN *looks in at window* L.) It's a big price Squire
Atwood pays. (*Looks out of window* R.) Ah, the tide is on the
ebb—and his body will go out to sea. (GIGGLE *begins to snore at
table.*) What's that? I'll go up stairs and see if the women folk

are asleep. (*Takes lamp from mantel at back, and goes towards* L. U. E.) And then—well then, I'll make my mind up.

Exit L. U. E. (*Lights down.*)

Gig. (*Waking up.*) Hullo! where the devil am I, and where the devil is my room? Everything is going round. I'm asleep—hic—it's too hot—hic—for—hic—me—hic—(*Rises and staggers towards door*, L. U. E.) This is my room.

Exit L. 2 E., *after taking off his shoes and leaving them near fireplace.*

Enter MULLIN *through window* L.

Mullin. (*At window.*) So far, all right. I'll take off my boots lest I make a noise—and I will steal a march on Clincher Katcraft.

Exit L. U. E, *after removing his shoes and leaving them near* GIGGLE'S.

Gig. (*Re-entering.*) I'll have another sour mash, if I fail in the attempt. (*Puts on one of his own and one of* MULLIN'S *shoes.*) I must put on my boots; my feet seem strange on this floor. Ha! ha! ha! This is hunting a sour mash in the dark. I wonder whether I'll stumble across any other mash.—(*Going to buffet, gets bottle and glass and* Exits L. 2 E., *laughing.*)

Enter HARLEY, *Window* L.

Harl. This jacket is wet again. (*Takes jacket off and places it on chair before fire, while speaking.*) I'll place it before the fire, while I see Elsie. (*Noise.*) Some one is coming.—(*Hides behind screen;* Enter CLINCHER *without light;* HARLEY *slips away through* L. U. E.

Clincher. It's all right. Now is the time. I'll throw him out of that window (*Pointing to window* R.), and he will fall into the water below and be carried out to sea. Why, he's coming this way. (*Sees* MULLIN, *who enters backwards. He puts on one of his own and one of* GIGGLE'S *shoes. A short struggle ensues, and* MULLIN *is stabbed and thrown out of window* R. *Splash is heard.*)

Clnch. Curse it, the sleeve of the jacket is torn, and it is Harley's. Here's mine.—(*Changes jacket by the fire, and puts on the other one.*)

Enter HARLEY, L. U. E. CLINCHER *hides behind screen.*

Harley. (*Putting on jacket removed by* CLINCHER.) I can't see Elsie! I wonder if my father is asleep? I'll see. Exit, L. U. E.

Clincher. What had induced that fellow to leave the light-house, and come here, I wonder? (*Knock heard at door*, L. U. E.) Who can that be ? Perhaps Mullin has changed his mind and returned. (*Goes and opens door.* Enter ATWOOD, R. U. E.) Ah, it's you, Squire! Hush! Harley, for some reason or other, has returned to the house. He is now in Latour's room.

Atwood. And he——

Clinch. Is at the bottom of the sea.

Atw. At last, the obstacle between me and fortune is no more. (Enter HARLEY, L. U. E.) He's here——

Harl. (L. C.) I wonder where my father can be?

Atw. (C.) Hello! What brings you here? I thought you were on duty at the light-house.

Harl. I came ashore to see Mr. Latour—my father.

Atw. And now that you have seen him, I presume you intend going back to your post.

Harl. But I haven't seen him. I have just come from his room, which is tenantless. The window is open and the place in confusion.

Atw. Answer me, why did **you** desert your post to visit Mr. Latour? (HARLEY *hesitates.*)

Clinch. I'll tell you, Squire. He went to Mr. Latour's room for the purpose of murdering him.

Harl. Tis false!

Clinch. See, there is blood on the sleeve of his jacket, and the cuff is torn.

Harl. I—I know nothing of it.

Clinch. Oh, yes, you do, for from that window (*Pointing* L.) I can swear I saw you strike Mr. Latour down and cast his body through that window (*Pointing* R.) into the sea.

Harl. 'Tis false!

Clinch. 'Tis true! Who, save you, can deny it?

Latour. (*Entering* R. U. E.) I—Joseph Latour!

Tableau.

LATOUR.

C.   HARLEY.

L. C.

CLINCHER,   ATWOOD.

R.   L.

Curtain.

ACT III.

Scene 1: *A Country Landscape in the 1st Grooves.*

Enter ATWOOD, L., *followed by* FIZZLES.

Atw. (C.) Fizzles, what does all this mean?

Fizzles. (L.) It's as plain as the nose on your face. The man who turned up alive in court is Michael Mullin, and not Joseph Latour at all. Mullin knows he's wanted; Mullin knows of this wonderful resemblance; and Mullin, finding Joseph Latour is murdered, wants to step into the dead man's shoes, and says that he is Joseph Latour.

Atw. Ah! I never thought of that.

Fiz. But I did; and I can swear this man is Michael Mullin.

Enter CLINCHER, L.

Clincher. (*On entering.*) Why, of course it is. (*Xes to* R.) I've just been before the judge in his chambers, and taken my affidavit that the man is Michael Mullin.

Fiz. Yes, and I've done the same. Here is the warrant for his apprehension on the charge of murder.

Clinch. (*Aside to* ATWOOD.) Have you brought me the other halves, as you promised?

Atw. (*Aside to* CLINCHER.) Yes, they are in my pocket. (*Takes bank-notes from pocket-book, and puts them into his side pocket.*) You shall have them directly. (*Direct to* FIZZLES.) I don't think he can have left the court yet, Fizzles; you mustn't lose him this time. Prove him to be Michael Mullin, bring this murder home to him, and obtain his conviction at any cost.

Fiz. Eh! You seem very anxious to convict.

Enter HARLEY *with* ELSIE, L.

Harley. No matter whom, so long as it is not himself. Ah, Squire Atwood, you laid your plans well—the husband killed, and the son convicted of his murder. You tried your best to send me to the scaffold; mind you do not find your way to it yourself.

Atw. I! Absurd.

Harl. Yes, you and your accomplice there.

Elsie. Hush! Harley, hush!

Clinch. I won't have my daughter associating with criminals. Come with me. (*Xes to* ELSIE, *who clings to* HARLEY *for protection.*)

Elsie. No, father, never! Henceforth Harley and I shall face the world.

Enter LATOUR, R.

Latour. (*Xing to* C.) Yes! but not as the penniless boatman, but as my son. Harley, my boy, your hand.

Harl. Father!

Lat. Look at the picture, Squire Atwood. Father and son united together. Be careful, Squire Atwood. When the truth shall become known, you perhaps, will stand more in fear of the hangman's rope than this boy who has been so foully accused.

Fiz. You can't hoodwink me with such bombastic talk. Look here, I must arrest you.

Lat. Arrest me! Where is your authority?

Fiz. (*Producing warrant.*) Here.

Lat. (*Looking over warrant.*) This is a warrant for the arrest of Michael Mullin.

Fiz. And you are Michael Mullin.

Lat. I!

Atw. Even you. It was a bold game to come into the Court and personate the dead. You obtained the freedom of this young man, but remember, both of you may have to go back to Court and give some better evidence as to your innocence.

Lat. Have a care, lest I cause you to give an account of your actions yesterday. I, at least can prove without a doubt, who and what I am.

Fiz. Come, Mr. Mullin, you are my prisoner.

Lat. Have a care Mr. Fizzles, the blunder you are about to commit may cost you your position. I clearly understand, Squire Atwood, the meaning of this arrest. You want to send me up to Sing-Sing to finish Mullin's sentence, and, if possible, get the fortune of the woman, who is your wife—the wife you tried to kill.

Atw. I! 'tis false.

Lat. No! I shall prove it yet—you bribed that ruffian there (*Pointing to* CLINCHER.) and his companion to loosen the bridge.

Atw. 'Tis a lie.

Lat. 'Tis true! I came into the room when Mullin had retired, unseen by you. I saw you give some of the bank-notes to Clincher there, and you gave the others to me, believing I was Mullin. Villains that you are, you were afraid to trust one another, and so you cut the notes in halves. One-half was paid before the crime, the other half to be paid after. I saw (*To* FIZZLES.) Squire Atwood put the other halves back into his breast pocket. In proof of what I say, ask him to show you his pocket-book, and doubtless you will find even now the corresponding halves of the notes.

Atw. In my pocket-book! (*Slips notes to* CLINCHER, *unseen.*) There is my pocket-book; see for yourself.

Fiz. (*Examining pocket-book.*) No, they are not there.

Enter GIGGLE, L.; *seizes* CLINCHER'S *arm and holds it up.*

Giggle. (L.) No! but they are here. Ha! ha! ha! (*Xes to* R. C.) There's the man that does the work, (*Pointing to* CLINCHER.) and there's the man that hired him. (*Points to Atwood.*)

Clinch. It's a lie! That man is Michael Mullin, and I can swear to it.

Gig. I can swear he isn't, and here's another who can swear the same.

Enter MADELINE, R.

Atw. Stay, madam—stay. I say that man is Michael Mullin—a convict. (*Aside to her.*) Beware! if you recognize him as Joseph Latour, your first husband, you prove yourself a bigamist, and as such you will be punished by the law. It is your choice—position and wealth with me—dishonor and disgrace with him.

Elsie. (*Going to her.*) Oh, speak, madam!

Madeline. Before the world I recognized in him, Joseph Latour, my husband.

Atw. This evidence is insufficient.

Gig. (R. C.) Let me make up the deficiency.

Atw. You, you laughing idiot!

Gig. No, the laugh is gone, and I am in earnest now—ha! ha! ha! in earnest—damn the laugh—I—I won't laugh, there—I know Michael Mullin, and that is not the man.

Clinch. Look out, Mr. Giggle, or your little forgery business will come to the surface.

Gig. It can't. Ha! ha!—Mullin is the only man who knew it. Mullin is dead, and the proofs died with him, and I—I—Augustus Giggle—won't stand by and see the ruin of an innocent man.

Atw. You! And what do you know?

Gig. A little too much for you—too much for Clincher. Look at this boot. (*Pulls up right leg of his trousers.*) I heard Clincher and Mullin plot the murder of Latour.

Clinch. It is a lie!

Gig. Oh, no it isn't. And the boot will prove it.

Atw. A boot! Absurd!

Gig. Ha! ha! ha! The boot. The night Mullin went to murder Latour, he took off his boots, and some how, in mistake, he put on one of mine, and I one of his. There it is! On the feet of the dead body you will find odd boots, one of mine and one of his own. Look at this, with the convict's number on it. (*Shows No. 17 on boot leg.*)

Fiz. True enough. This is Michael Mullin's boot.

Gig. Yes! but the boot is much too large for that man's foot. (*Referring to* LATOUR.) This boot is cut for a bunion—look there, and if it fits him I'll be hanged, as sure as Clincher Katcraft will——

Clinch. All rubbish! How was it the body found was wearing Latour's clothes.

Gig. That's a thing I don't know.

Lat. But I do. I had been drugged, but only partly so. My clothes were on the chair—Mullin came into my room, put mine on, and left his own. Hearing a noise, he went outside to see what it was. Seeing that foul play was meant, though half stupefied, I knew I was powerless against two men, both armed. I took the clothes he left and escaped by the window, while Clincher evidently mistook Mullin for me and killed him.

Clinch. (*Aside.*) This is getting too hot for me.

Fiz. You'll have to come before the presiding judge and make an affidavit of this. I don't feel disposed to act otherwise in the matter.

Mad. Joseph! I have some letters and papers which may be of service to you. I will bring them. Elsie, come with me. (*Xes* L.)

Atw. So, Madam, you return to my home again?

Mad. For the last time. Fayette Atwood, for years I have been the silent uncomplaining victim of your cruelty, but now a happier and better time has come, and Heaven grant that in this great wide world we may never meet again. Farewell for ever!

Exit *with* ELSIE, L. I E.

Atw. (*Aside to* CLINCHER.) Quick, Clincher, don't lose sight of them. We have a bold and dangerous game to play—the stakes, our lives—follow them.

Clinch. (*Aside to him.*) If you hear me whistle, come to me.

Exit, L. I E.

Harl. (*Aside, following* CLINCHER *unseen.*) I shall not lose sight of you, Clincher Katcraft. Exit, L. I E.

Fiz. (*To* LATOUR.) As to you, sir, I have one clue by which you can easily prove whether you are Michael Mullin or Joseph Latour, and here it is (*Producing letter from pocket*) ; a letter in the undoubted handwriting of Joseph Latour, written, on the day of the murder, to his bankers in New York. Give me a specimen of your handwriting. If it is the same, you are Joseph Latour, and if it is not, you are Michael Mullin. (*Shows letter from pocket-book.*)

Lat. I can easily do that. (*Takes out memorandum and writes in it, then shows it to* FIZZLES.) There, sir, is my handwriting.

Fiz. (*Compares them.*) And it is not the same.

Gig. No, of course it isn't ; but this is, ha! ha! ha!

Fiz. (*Taking letter from* GIGGLE.) What is this?

Gig. The original letter which was written by Joseph Latour—taken by the boy, Sammy—copied by Michael Mullin—torn up by Clincher, picked up by Mrs. Katcraft, and pasted together by me. (*To* LATOUR.) Hang me, if I am not your good angel, and I only want a pair of wings and a night-gown to look like one!

Lat. (*Pointing to letter* GIGGLE *had.*) This is my handwriting, and will correspond to the letter Mrs. Atwood has. You see, Squire, the truth is coming out. (*A whistle call is heard from* L.)

Atw. (*Aside.*) The signal from Clincher! I must gain time. (*Direct, to* FIZZLES.) It is not for you to decide who this man is, but to take him into custody on that warrant. It is your duty to arrest him, and for his keeping, I hold you responsible. Exit, L.

Fiz. Oh, hang it all ; I don't know what to do !

Enter MRS. KATCRAFT, R.

Mrs. Katcraft. Oh, detective ! Oh, Mr. Giggle ! That husband of mine and Squire Atwood, I'm sure, are up to some mischief. Mrs. Atwood left to go up to her house and hasn't returned, and Clincher, I believe, has waylaid her and taken her to the lighthouse to murder her.

Fiz. Murder her ! What makes you think so ?

Mrs. K. I heard him whisper to Squire Atwood. Oh, don t stand staring there, but go at once, or there'll be murder !

Fiz. I begin to see it all, but I must have authority to act upon. I know my game. You, sir, (*To* LATOUR.) come with me.

Lat. There's no time to be lost.

Fiz. You gentlemen armed ?

Lat. I have right and justice on my side, and they are the best weapons in the world.   *Exit with* FIZZLES, L.

Gig. Now I can have my laugh out. Ha! ha! ha! (*Going* L.) It reminds me of my wife catching me kissing another man's wife for novelty. Come along, Mrs. Katcraft, I'm afraid you'll have to get another husband. I'm in the market you know. (*Going off* L., *laughing.*)

Mrs. K. (*Following.*)   Heaven, be praised ! the man's half-witted.   Exit, L.

Scene 2. *Storage room on the ground floor of the light-house. At rise of Curtain, Music, tremolo.* Enter CLINCHER *and* ATWOOD, *Door* L. C., *carrying* MADELINE, *fainting ; they lay her down upon canvas cot* R., *up stage.*

Clincher. It's all right.   No one has seen us; we can leave her here till the tide's on the ebb, and then do our work and be off.

Atwood. (C.) Curse that fellow, Giggle ! the information he will give in this affair, to the authorities, will be the means of our arrest.   We had better take to foreign parts, before it is too late.

Clinch. (L. C.)   I have something to do before I can go.

Atw. You! what ?

Clinch. My little honest savings.   There's many a gold watch and silver spoon the owners didn't give me—and a few handsome patterns of silk which I ain't a going to leave for my blessed wife and undutiful daughter.

Atw. Let us go outside and see if the coast is clear.　I'm sure no one has seen us.　　　　　　　　**Exit,** *with* CLINCHER, L. C.

　　　　　Enter HARLEY, *door,* L. 2 E.

Harley. No one but me; (*Coming* C.)　So all is discovered, eh? And they intend flying from justice.　I wonder what it was they carried from shore?　No doubt some of the plunder of which Clincher spoke.　How to prevent their escape—ah, their boat!— I'll cast it adrift.　Ha! ha! ha! the villians little dream they are caught like rats in a trap.　　　　　　　　　　**Exit,** L. C

　　Re-enter ATWOOD *and* CLINCHER, *door,* R. 2 E.

Madeline. (*Waking.*)　Where am I?　(ATWOOD *goes to table* R. C. *down stage, pours out water into glass from jug and returns to her, speaking all the while.*)

Atwood. Where you should be, with your husband at the light-house of Barnegat.　(CLINCHER *is seen looking off, out of window,* C.)

Mad. I remember now, you met me on the road—seized me and I—oh—(*Swoons.*)

Atw. (*Going towards* CLINCHER.)　The effects of the drug have not passed away.　(*At window.*)　How's the tide?

Clinch. On the ebb.　We won't have to wait long to dispose of her.

Atw. (*Pointing off* R., *out of window.*)　What light is that burn-ing?

Clinch. It means all right ; the lights are worked with levers in the room above.　No. 1 lever turns on a white light—that means all right.　No. 2 turns on a red light—that's a danger signal, and is turned on when assistance is needed from the shore.　If I were to turn on the red light, the life saving station would bring assist-ance here in ten minutes.　(MADELINE *slightly revives.*)

Atw. (*At side of cot.*)　Hush! see, she is reviving.

Mad. Why am I brought here?

Atw. You hold in your name and to your account one hundred thousand dollars, which I cannot touch without your authority. Awkward circumstances compel me to leave the country.

Clinch. (*Down* C.)　Very awkward circumstances.

Atw. But before going, you must do me a favor.　Sign this document.　(*Produces document.*)

Mad. (*Rising in cot.*) Document! let me see it.

Atw. (*Giving it to her.*) Merely an authority from you to your bankers to withdraw and hand over to me the bonds and other easily convertible securities which are lodged there in your name, and which I at once will turn into cash.

Mad. What would you do?

Atw. Take your money and leave for Europe, and never return to America again.

Mad. (*Rising from cot.*) And what if I refuse?

Atw. I shall have to kill you first and forge it afterwards. Come, your signature.

Mad. Never! I will not beggar my son for the sake of a villian like you.

Atw. Then, your life! (*Rushing at her.*)

Mad. (*With defiance.*) Take it!

Clinch. (c. *interposing.*) Give her a little time to think. I've got my valuables to pack, and you must help me. If I lend you a hand with your plundering job, you must lend me a hand with mine.

Atw. (R. C.) Be it so; but we can't leave her here alone.

Clinch. (*Producing rope.*) Lend me a hand to bind her—(*They lash her to cot.*)

Mad. Cruel and remorseless villains, not satisfied with my death, you would tortue——

Clinch. (*Finishing tying* MADELINE.) Theie, that's all right.

Atw. That is a strange knot.

Clinch. Yes! it's a knot the devil himself couldn't untie—unless he knew the secret, and nobody knows that but myself and Elsie.

Exeunt both L. C., *up stage.*

Enter ELSIE, R. 2 E.

Elsie. And Elsie means to do it.

Mad. Eh!

Elsie. Courage, Madame. After I left you I came here with Harley, who will soon return. (*Unties knot as she is speaking.*) We were here together, when we saw Clincher and Mr. Atwood in the boat—but we did not know that you were with them. (*Supporting* MADELINE *to window.*)

Mad. He must hasten or he will be too late. Ah, the signals! (*Looking out of window.*)

Elsie. I understand them. You hide behind those (*Pointing* L., *near* L. 2 E.) coils of rope while I go and put on the red light for assistance from shore. (MADELINE *hides behind coils of rope near* L. 2 E. ELSIE *Exits* L. 2 E.)

Enter CLINCHER and ATWOOD, L. C.

Atwood. (*Going towards cot.*) Now then, your answer?

Clincher. Damn it! she's gone.

Atw. She must have released herself.

Clinch. I'll take my oath she never untied that knot.

Atw. (*Sees* MADELINE.) Ah! there she is. (*He pursues her about stage; she screaming.*)

Mad. Help! help! (*At window looking out.*) Ah! the boat has gone. (CLINCHER *and* ATWOOD *seize her.*)

Clinch. Ah, you will not escape us so easily.

Atw. (*Looking out of window.*) Look! look there! (*Pointing out of window* R.); *the danger signal!*

Clinch. (*As he is going off.*) Curse it! I'll have it down in a jiffy. Bind her to those coils of rope. (*Pointing* R.; ATWOOD *binds her, while Clincher goes off* L. 2 E.)

Atw. Aye! as tight as Clincher did. You'll not escape this time. (*Ties her to coils of rope* R.) Ah, my pretty one, you had better consent to my wish. The tide has began to ebb fast and your time is drawing nigh.

Mad. Monster!

Atw. Will you sign the paper?

Mad. Never!

ELSIE rushes on through L. 2 E., and hides behind rope L. CLINCHER Enters L. 2 E., much excited. ELSIE disappears L. 2 E.

Atw. (C.) Have you removed the danger signal?

Clinch. (L. C.) Yes, no fear of it again.

Atw. (*Looking and pointing* R. *out of window.*) Look there!

Clinch. The place is haunted, or there's some one there—man, woman, or devil, let them look to themselves. (*Draws knife, rushes to* L. 2 E. ELSIE *holds door;* CLINCHER *breaks it open and enters.* ELSIE *rushes out, pursued by* CLINCHER *with drawn knife; he seizes her at* L. C. *Door, and drags her down* C.) What jade are you that dares to run things here?

Atw. (R.)   Kill her.

Clinch. (*Dragging her down* C.)   I mean to—(*Struggle ensues ;* CLINCHER *raises knife—about to stab* ELSIE—*but recoils in blank amazement.*)   Damn it, my daughter!

Atw. (*To* MADELINE.)   Will you sign?

Mad. Never!

Atw. Take her Clincher and throw her out of the window. The tide is now strong enough to take her out to sea.   (CLINCHER *and* ATWOOD *lift her and carry her up stage* C.; *they are about to throw her out when* HARLEY *appears at window, through which he* enters.   CLINCHER *and* ATWOOD *drop* MADELINE, *who falls into the arms of* LATOUR, *who* enters L. C., *accompanied by* MRS. KATCRAFT *and* FIZZLES, *who handcuffs* CLINCHER.   GIGGLE *unfastens* MADELINE, *while a struggle ensues between* LATOUR *and* ATWOOD.   *During the struggle,* ATWOOD *attempts to shoot* LATOUR, *but shoots himself.*

Tableau.

FIZZLES with CLINCHER. •   ATWOOD, dead on Stage.

up R.   *up* L.

LATOUR and MADELINE.

C.

HARLEY embracing ELSIE.   GIGGLE and MRS. KATCRAFT.

R. C.   L. C.

Latour. (C. *to* MADELINE.)   Now that the dark clouds have vanished, and sunshine looms in our path, I have one request to make—that you will forgive the past, and never recall the sad incidents of one who was "SAVED FROM THE WRECK."

Curtain.